HOLDING A WITCH

A SPRING EQUINOX ROMANCE

LAUREN CONNOLLY

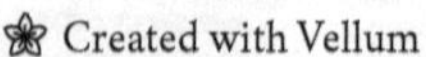 Created with Vellum

For the bees

CONTENT WARNING

This book contains scenes discussing weight loss/malnutrition, captivity, manipulative relationships, and loss of a parent.

DENTON

*B*ears should never be tasked with setting up witch altars. Harriet's first blunder is the thrift store table, whose back right leg is one centimeter shorter than the rest. Every time my sister places another object on the unstable surface, I tense for the collection of items to go tumbling across our backyard.

"Honey," she mutters to herself, hustling by me and disappearing into the house to find premium Bluebell honey.

The nectar is harvested from our family's own hives, blessed by the Earth Mother and coveted by both the magical and human community.

The idea of our bees' hard work spilling onto the ground decides it for me. I level the table by wedging a flat rock under the leg.

There, I helped. Now, it's time to walk away and stop pretending bear shifters can work witch magic.

When my sister returns to set a mason jar of honey in the

middle of the other items, she double-checks her notes, squinting to read in the dim predawn light, which mutes the normally vibrant aqua color of her dyed hair.

"What am I missing?"

When a few seconds go by with her face scrunched in confusion, I relent again.

"Flowers."

"Ah! Yes. You're right." Harriet grins my way, the joyous expression brighter than the approaching sunrise. "She's coming back this time, Denton. I'm sure of it."

All I can manage in response is a grunt. If I open my mouth, I'll end up pointing out she said the same thing on the winter solstice. And Mabon. And Litha before that. When disappointment comes once more, my sister will easily convince herself that her best friend will show up at the very next holiday and maintain that optimism for decades, if need be.

While I silently stew in my own doubt.

Why couldn't Cordelia have chosen a return date before she left?

What would I have done if she had and that date came and passed?

Harriet takes my noncommittal noise as tacit agreement, humming as she bustles back to the house. Despite the now-flat surface, the altar still has a haphazard air.

"Ostara calls for balance," a voice murmurs in my memory.

Shouldn't the altar reflect that? I reason. My hands reach forward, as if guided by another force.

Yellow beeswax candles on the left, green nettle candles on the right.

Jar of honey on the left, glass of milk on the right.

Lemons on the left, limes on the right.

I step back just as Harriet reappears, two flowerpots cradled in her arms. She pauses in front of the altar, taking in the new arrangement, and then she does the smart thing and hands me the flowers.

Forsythia on the left, lilacs on the right.

"Almost perfect. We just need the eggs." Harriet rummages in her pockets.

"You're carrying raw eggs in your pants? That's a hazard waiting to happen."

"You are so grumpy this morning. You should be excited! Cordelia will be here soon!" Her hands come up with two plastic eggs. The kind that children think a massive rabbit somehow produces and hides for them.

Ah, blissful ignorance. How I miss it.

Despite my doubt, I keep my negativity tucked behind a stoic mask. Harriet's massive pockets produce a few more items, and I accept the egg, a slip of paper, and a pen when she passes them to me.

"What now?"

These are witch traditions, which makes them new to us both. Growing up in a family of shifters, we mainly celebrated the changing of seasons with large meals and family. Now, with our parents passed on and relatives moved away, Harriet and I are all that's left.

Unless we can guide Cordelia back to us today.

"*Write a wish, put it in the egg, put the egg on the altar,*" my sister reads aloud the neatly written instructions Cordelia transcribed for her over a year ago. "Sounds easy enough."

Sounds too easy to do anything helpful. Shouldn't traveling between realms require more than plastic eggs?

Still, I follow the instructions and write a single sentence.

Come home.

With neat creases, I fold the paper into a minuscule square, close the note in the egg, and rest the desperate hope on the honey side of the altar. If Harriet had asked to see it, I would have shown her. If I read her wish, I'm sure the words would read along the same sentiment.

"That's everything." Harriet sets her egg next to the milk and steps back, her movements muffled by the spongy grass, wet with pre-morning dew. "Now, we just wait for her to get here."

Like we've been doing since the moment she left.

Harriet settles in a folding lawn chair, but I choose to sit on the ground. As the grass crushes into the dirt under me, I hope to feel something other than the dampness soaking through the butt of my pants. If Cordelia were here, she would tell us about the magic filling the earth and the air, stronger today more than most. With her detailed descriptions, I would sense the magic in a way shifters never had before.

She was never shy about sharing the secrets of witches.

The past tense of my thoughts bothers me. Cordelia Vetle exists only in my past even though these present actions are for her.

Will she be in my future?

Harriet would lovingly berate me if I spoke the doubtful thought out loud. Even now, my sister shifts and fidgets with eagerness, as if we were traveling a winding road and Cordelia only waited around the next bend, her hand raised in a wave, her plush mouth curved in a secret grin, hinting at stories to tell of her adventures.

But why would a woman who could travel to all the worlds in existence want to come back to a small house in Roanoke, Virginia? What appeal would two orphaned bear shifters hold?

An ache starts up behind my eyes, and I realize I've been staring hard at the altar without blinking for a good five minutes. Letting my lids drop, I once again remind myself that high hopes mean more misery at the end of this day.

In an act of self-preservation, I shift my attention to the woods that brush against the back edge of our property. The space between the trunks fades into ominous shadows in the dim light. A warning not to wander into their depths, for risk of losing yourself. Many days, I wish I could disconnect from my body and disappear into those shadows. Maybe then the pain in my heart wouldn't plague me.

"Look!"

At Harriet's gasp, I whip my attention to the altar, leaning forward, searching frantically for brown hair as soft as the fuzz of a bumblebee, and eyes as green as new spring leaves, and a smile that sits higher on the left curve than the right.

None of those sights appear. All that has changed in the last moment is the addition of delicate yellow wings fluttering among our offerings.

After a year of practice, I still struggle against the battering pain of disappointment.

"My butterflies like it." Harriet unscrews the top to her thermos, releasing the scent of honeysuckle coffee—her homemade brew—into the cool, humid air. "That has to be a good sign." She swallows a large gulp of hot caffeine that she doesn't need.

Butterflies like flowers. It's not a divine sign, the cynical part of my brain responds.

"Yeah," I say.

Harriet throws me an eager, grateful smile. Unlike many big brothers, I've never found joy in the teasing of my younger sister. Even when we were only cubs, I always wanted to be the one pushing her stroller, or feeding her mashed berries and honey, or reading her bedtime stories.

Perhaps the gods were preparing us for the day when our family of four would become a family of two.

When Cordelia was here, we felt like a family of three.

The sky in the eastern horizon lightens from navy to periwinkle, heralding the new day.

"Sunrise on the Ostara is a powerful time." The hushed voice strokes through my memory, twined into my brain cells on a day like this years ago. Cordelia had her arm hooked through mine, her other wrapped around Harriet's waist as we watched the sky lighten. *"The beginning of a balanced day. Can you feel it?"*

With her, I could.

Without her …

A buzzing seeps from the ground, vibrating through my body and raising the hairs on my skin.

"Do you feel that?" Harriet's voice squeaks on the last word, but I'm too busy surging toward the altar to answer.

Above the collection of innocent offerings, the air rends in two, strands of light dangling like torn threads along the edges of the chasm. Through the portal, I spy the hazy purple of a twilight sky and towering white rock formations. An alien landscape.

Then, a figure, the form familiar, hurtles toward the opening.

"Cordelia!" My sister's shout cracks through the air just as the edges of the portal begin to knit together.

"No!" The word roars out of me, and I'm there, reaching my arm into another world, skin scalding in protest as I pierce the veil.

But the burn means nothing when a cool, callous palm clasps mine. With a mighty tug, I heave the witch through the opening, into our world.

Into my chest.

Into my heart, the one place she never left.

We fall to the ground, tangled in each other, and I enfold her in my arms, mapping every point of her that presses against me.

The witch's once-rounded curves have more angles, more hard edges. But my body would know hers, no matter the subtle alterations. My DNA has magnetized to hers, the cells reforming to create space for hers to fit into.

Hair tickles my nose, smelling of familiar sage and foreign scents I cannot catalog. A chill clings to the edges of her, as if she stepped out of a frigid winter. Her breaths, deep and ragged, hold the same pitch as they always have, and I could listen to an orchestra of her breathing for the rest of my life.

Then, Cordelia laughs. "Denton."

Those two sounds are the crescendo of the symphony.

"Cor." My whisper, harsh with disbelief, drifts off with the rise of the sun. "You're back."

She isn't lost. She isn't dead. She hasn't found a new home in another realm, never to return to ours.

She's here.

"Of course she is." Harriet crouches beside our prone forms, bending awkwardly to add her arms to the welcoming hug. "I told you she would be."

2

CORDELIA

e made it home.

Burying my head in the cotton of Denton's T-shirt as we lie on the ground, I suck in lungfuls of his honey scent, mixed with the cedar tang of his aftershave and a musky twinge of clean fur.

Gods, I've missed the smell of this bear.

Then, Harriet presses close, and I smell honeysuckle and bear. I bite back a sob. Instead, I coax a smile onto my face and raise my head to take in the sight of them both.

My best friend dyed her hair since I last saw her. What was formerly a solid mass of bubblegum pink is now a fascinating combination of blues and greens. Her dark eyes twinkle under a set of sharp bangs and above a cluster of familiar freckles, light-brown speckles standing out on her pale skin.

"Did you miss me?" Harriet tilts her colorful head, and I have to force away the urge to cry again.

"So much."

"And me?"

The question melts through my skin. The deep tone both a pain and a relief, like a skillful elbow pressed into a muscle that's been tight for *years*.

I meet another set of dark eyes, these under thick black brows and above cheekbones that are sharper than I remember. But maybe they only appear that way because of the dense onyx beard that claims the lower half of a face that used to be clean-shaven.

While the facial hair could be considered attractive, I mourn the loss of his entire familiar face. Desperation fuels my fingers as I reach my hands up and delve under the coarse hair until I find the shape of his jaw. But I'm not satisfied until the pad of my thumb locates the subtle dip at the point of his chin. The slightly off-center cleft I've spent days tracing in my mind.

"So, you *are* Denton."

The furry mass on his face creases with a smile.

"Could never fool you."

"Look at your clothes!" Harriet plucks at the fabric of my ornate jacket. "And your hair! It's grown so long. Was it really three … wait. Um, is your bag *moving*?"

A disgruntled string of clicks and chirps answers my friend's question. Allowing my hands to drop away from Denton's face, I carefully unbutton the satchel slung across my chest. I fashioned the carrier myself, the outside formed of the toughest leather and the inside cushioned with wool.

But the most comfortable sack is still a sack, and my passenger wants out.

"Good eye." I pop the final button and pull back the top flap. "Harriet, Denton, say hello to the newest member of my family. This is Honey."

A head the size of an apple emerges, revealing pebbled

golden skin covering a reptilian face. A forked tongue sneaks out in quick jabs as my companion scents the air.

"Oh Goddess. It's beautiful. Look at that color. Pure gold. Where'd you get them?"

I move to sit up to take my weight off of Denton, but he shifts with me, keeping his arms in a loose circle around my waist. The continued contact helps soothe the adrenaline still lingering in my veins.

"Honey is a *druzvel*." I pronounce the foreign word as best I can, still not managing the proper accent after all this time. "He's a type of lizard. A rare one. And he found me." I place my palm flat in front of his nose, and he clasps my skin gently in his claws and pulls himself out of the carrier. "He's my familiar."

Harriet's delighted gasp almost drowns out a cluster of Honey's curious whistles. Instead of climbing up to his favorite perch on my shoulder, the little golden creature creeps his kitten-sized body down to my lap and then onto Denton's arm. The *druzvel* scents the bear shifter's skin, and I wonder if he breathes in the same sweet, husky combo I did.

"Your sojourn to the realm was successful then." Denton holds still, letting the lizard examine him.

Successful. Yes, it was that. My journey was many things.

Not all of them good.

"I know you probably want to hear everything." I meet Harriet's eager eyes, unable to suppress an answering smile. "But can you give me some time to recalibrate?"

"Of course. No problem. Are you hungry? Tired?"

An itch I learned to ignore long ago resurfaces suddenly, and I have to twine my fingers together to keep from unbuttoning my jacket.

"Honestly, the first thing I want to do is put on different clothes. Do you have any I can borrow?"

A short while later, I'm in my own pair of decadently soft

sweatpants, plus a well-worn T-shirt, both pulled from a duffel I forgot I'd left at the Bluebells' house. My hands disappear into the long sleeves of a hoodie Denton put on me himself, all while Honey clung to his broad shoulder.

My familiar approves of the bear.

When I took off the tight-fitting, intricately crafted clothes I'd traveled home in, I considered lighting a fire and burning the itchy woollike garments. Instead, I neatly folded them and tucked the stack in a far corner of a closet in one of the guest rooms, leaving them there to be ignored until I can handle mentally revisiting them.

The rising sun spills across the yard, and I sprint out, barefoot, to stand in the rays, soaking up the heated glow.

"Is this your way of saying you want to hang out outside?" Harriet follows with a steaming mug of green tea, handing me the warm drink.

In the rising vapor, I catch tart notes of lemon and sweet honey, no doubt harvested from the Bluebells' own hives.

"Perpetual twilight gets old real fast." I sink into a cross-legged seat in the middle of the grass. "Catch me up. What did I miss?"

Harriet, ever the busybody, doesn't sit beside me, instead slipping on a set of cloth gloves and going to work on tugging weeds from a nearby garden. "You know you've been gone a year, right?"

I nod, glancing at my wrist, where a thick leather cuff sits, firmly holding two watch faces.

"How long was it for you?" She tosses a dandelion in a nearby basket.

"They measured in ... I guess it translates into *turnings*. I spent two and a half turnings there. But that was three years, just about."

Time works differently across realms.

Harriet huffs. "You're older than me now." She pulls a set

of shears out of her overall pockets and neatly clips a snow-drop at its base before leaning over to pass me the flower. "I'm sorry we missed so many of your birthdays. You'll be … thirty-three next time? In two months? We'll do something big. Get you a bouncy castle."

A shadow falls over me as I chuckle. When I glance up, I find Denton and Honey have joined us. The big man keeps his face impassive as he crouches and carefully sets my animal companion in my lap.

Realization locks me in a frozen silence. The bear shifter handling the *druzvel* so carefully doesn't surprise me. But the ease with which I left Honey in his care does.

Recently, I used every bit of my will and magic to cling to my familiar.

And I handed him off to Denton without thought or worry.

"Thank you," I manage to press through my suddenly stiff lips.

Denton only offers me a blackberry scone in response. A dangerously large lump forms in my throat, and I worry I won't be able to eat the delicious gift. When he moves to stand, most likely to leave me be, I drop the flower and pastry in my lap—only keeping hold of my scalding tea—to clutch his hand.

"The realm of Meztra doesn't have bears."

The last thing I want to ask, after Denton and Harriet have done so much for me, is for more from him. But I can't help the subtle plea in my voice.

I need you.

The dense black beard crinkles with another hint of a smile, and his thick fingers give mine an understanding squeeze before slipping from my grasp.

Denton reaches behind his head, clasping the neck of his shirt and removing it in one smooth tug that sets all my nerves to clenching. Ever since grade school, he's been a big man. But after I lived with only lean individuals for so long, his mass assaults my gaze and leaves me sucking in a steadying breath. Black hair covers a meaty chest, thinning over his stomach but still drawing the eye downward.

With deft fingers, he undoes his belt, not bothering to slip the leather from the loops before his thumb seeks out the button at the top of his fly.

A good friend would drop her eyes.

But I was never *that* good.

Denton turns at the last moment—right as the denim and briefs drag down his thighs—blocking his front while giving me a glorious view of his behind. Before I can take my time in admiring the pale globes, the air condenses around him, and the shape of an animal overtakes his body.

Thick, dark fur covers his massive form, which weighs maybe a hundred pounds more than a real black bear. Still close enough to fool a human who might catch a glimpse. Gray eyes rest above a long snout and below a fuzzy set of ears I've always found entirely too adorable.

The bear shifter shakes off the effects of his change while I recover from the intimate glimpse I've longed for what seems my whole life.

I can never recall the exact moment I fell in love with Denton Bluebell, but I know I was at least five years old before it happened.

Because that's how old I was when my mother enrolled me in his parents' day care. The first day she left me in their care, I sat by the front window, watching the street and silently pining for her to come pick me up. Then, a big, furry body settled next to me, and without thinking, I leaned on the mass and fell asleep. When I woke up, a girl with dark, tangled hair was watching me while popping blackberries into her mouth, the juices staining her fingers.

. . .

"That's Denton," the girl said, pointing with a berry-smeared finger at the bear I was using as a pillow. "My big brother. I'm the only one who gets to nap with him."

My teeth bit into my bottom lip as I tried to stop the tears threatening to fall. The bear grunted, puffing out a warm breath that rustled my hair.

"But it's okay." The girl held out the bowl of fruit in offering. "You can nap with him too. But we have to be best friends. We have to pretend we're sisters. Then, he can be your brother too."

Since then, Harriet has always been my best friend, bordering on an adopted sister.

But Denton has never felt like my brother, even as I let that impression exist on the surface.

In my heart though, I love him differently. Deeply and with a passion that burns so hot that I often wince at the thought of what we could be if my fantasies melded with reality.

For now though, I'll content myself with the subtle warmth of his animal form settling at my back, once again acting as a support for me to rest my body on. I sink into the familiar fur as I sip my tea and eat my pastry. Honey curls up on my knee and eats the petals of my birthday flower.

Meanwhile, Harriet weeds her garden and cheerfully relates the celebrity gossip I missed while I was away. A light topic I can half-listen to as I soak in the sunshine and enjoy the rise and fall of Denton's rib cage.

Tension that slowly overtook my body—a tight worry that gripped me until I found myself caught in a noose—only now begins to ease enough for me to breathe. Finally, I can fill my lungs to capacity. I count out the seconds as I suck in oxygen. Proving with each inhale how loose my chest becomes while soaked in love.

"Harry?" I interrupt the latest saga of a music artist's rereleased album causing an uproar.

"Yeah?"

"Could you sing something?" My eyelids droop, but I'm scared to fall asleep. Denton's sides expand and contract with his inhales and exhales, the motion rocking me. "I haven't heard music in … so long."

"They didn't sing there?"

My mind revisits stiff, upholstered seats and haunting ethereal notes. "Not like we do here."

Harriet shrugs, wearing her familiar pleased grin. My friend loves her singing voice but is too modest about how well she can play with the notes of others' songs. One of her favorite musicians is Billy Joel, so I'm not surprised when she chooses from his catalog.

As I welcome the long-missed daylight and revel in the soft cotton against my skin and the warm bear at my back, Harriet lets her voice drift through a song about Vienna and how the place will always wait for me.

In some trivia-winning corner of my mind, I know the lyrics comment on growing older. But every time she sings the last chorus line, I cannot help hearing different words. A teasing promise.

"When will you realize … the Bluebells wait for you …"

3

DENTON

I smell her tears before I see them.

As Harriet serenades us, the scent of salt pairs with sage. Tilting my massive head, I examine Cordelia from the corner of my eye. Wet trails trace over her gaunt cheeks. A year ago, she had a cushiony layer on her body that begged to have fingers gently pressing, and lips sucking, and teeth nipping into her. A year ago, the sun painted freckles on her skin every day and soaked into her cells until she glowed, even in the darkest night.

Curving my spine, I curl more tightly around our witch, worried the chill on this first day of spring will pierce straight to her bones.

Why is she crying?

Thoughts form slower in my mind when I take on my clawed form, but that question is the first of a string to pummel me.

Why is she hurting?

How can I stop it?

How can I be everything she needs without destroying myself the next time she leaves?

As if sensing my distress, the strange golden lizard climbs off his witch's lap and scuttles to the space in front of my nose. Intelligent, marble-patterned eyes meet mine before a series of clicks and chirps rattle from between his small, sharp teeth.

"He's talking to you," Cordelia murmurs low enough that she doesn't interrupt my sister, who drifts into a country song. "Do you understand what he's saying?"

Unfortunately, the act of turning into an animal doesn't give me the ability to converse with them. Cordelia is the master of languages. Last count, she knew six spoken on Earth and three spoken in different realms. As a traveling witch, she made a point to study the places she wanted to visit.

That's what she told us when she was eighteen, packing a bag to go stay with her aunt in Maine. Another traveling witch who could train her not only to transport herself to other realms, but to also survive in them once she got there. That was the first time I lost Cordelia, when she went north to study. At least then, we were able to text, and visit, and video-chat during the time she was gone.

The second time she left, she truly *left*, and I panicked.

For four months and seven days, Cordelia removed herself from this earthly plane to travel in the Realm of Jorval. It didn't matter that she'd told us she was going. It didn't matter that the passage of time differed only slightly. It didn't matter that Jorval was the most common realm traveling witches went to.

All I could think about was how no matter what I did, I had no way to see her. No way to tell if she was alive and well.

When she returned from that trip, I hugged her close and told her I missed her. Then—once she was settled, fed, and talking about her next trip—I walked into the woods, climbed a tree, and shuddered as helpless tears fell.

Two years later, Cordelia left again for another realm.

Within days, Harriet claimed I was impossible to live with and started a Growl Jar. I owed the jar a quarter every time I snapped or grumbled at her or anyone else. When I filled it in a week's time, she got a bigger jar. After that overflowed, my sister used the change to buy a punching bag. The next jar went to buying me therapy sessions.

Those helped some.

But nothing brought Cordelia back, except for time. Then, the calendar days became my enemies as they counted down her next departure.

Let's pause here. Right now.

Years ago, I acknowledged that even though I loved Cordelia more than any other being could, my stationary existence meant I would never be her partner. That our embraces would never transform from friendship to passion. That she loved me and Harriet the same. We were her safe harbor, where she continued to return.

She needs me and misses me, but she doesn't tangle herself in sweat-soaked sheets, calling out my name as her hands coax pleasure from her body, wishing my palms were the ones stroking her sensitive spots.

If Cordelia fell in love with another on Earth and chose to stay with them always rather than travel to another realm again, I could live an uncomfortably content existence. My heart would always ache from the unhealed edges left after I tore out a chunk of the sensitive organ and tucked the piece in her pocket before I was old enough to build protective walls. But I would know where she was, and how she was, and most importantly, that she was safe and happy.

If that person who could keep her here exists, she hasn't met them yet. And without them, Cordelia loves her magic and her freedom to explore more than anything. The day will come when she disappears once more, and I'll wait with Harriet's unshaken optimism, burning bright beside the inescapable shadow of my terror.

Honey chirps at me again. The noise doesn't translate into words, but the familiar's attention pulls me away from my future fears and into the present.

She's here now. Live in the moment with her. Make her happy while you can. Give her a reason to always come home.

Droplets cling to Cordelia's dark lashes as others continue to flow downward. Lifting my head from the soft grass, I use my large snout to snuffle her hair, and then I reach out a long purple tongue and slurp it up her face, tasting the salt of her tears and loving her sharp gasp, followed by bubbling laughter.

"Denton! Gross!" She pushes on my neck, trying to shove me away, but I have hundreds of pounds on her and a mission to hear her laugh some more.

I lick her again, and she shrieks and tries to hide her face inside my hoodie. I bundled her into the massive garment because an illogical part of my brain reasoned that if she's wearing my clothes, then she's tethered to me, and she can't slip through another crack in the air.

Seemingly happy with my actions, Honey leaves off staring and trundles over to Harriet's side. The strange creature lifts its flat, spiny head to snap at the occasional butterfly that drifts too close.

"No, Honey. We like the butterflies. Why don't you find a cricket? Or here. Try these."

My sister grabs a handful of dandelions from her basket and drops the yellow weeds in front of the familiar. A forked tongue sneaks out, sampling the air, and then the reptile chomps down on the plant.

"I was going to put those in a salad, but have as many as you want." Harriet glances toward us over her shoulder. "He can eat them, right?"

Cordelia straightens off me, her face going serious, the corners of her mouth pinching. "I'm not sure. He normally eats plants and small bugs, but they were different than the ones we have here." Uncertainty curls through her voice. A note of insecurity I'm not used to hearing from the confident witch.

Is it because she's concerned for her familiar, or is there more I'm not seeing?

Why was she crying?

"Does Fenella still live in town?" Cordelia names another local witch who works a day job as a vet.

"I saw her at the store a few weeks ago. No mention of moving. I think I have her number." Harriet pulls her cell out of a deep pocket. "Want me to text her?"

"Yes. Thank you." Cordelia rises to her feet and gathers Honey in her arms.

Since I'm no longer needed as back support, I shift to my human form and reach for my clothes.

A heavy weight settles on my bare skin, and I glance back to find Cordelia watching me. She did that before when I stripped.

Could she want to see me naked?

More like she's been surrounded by other realm beings for so long that a human body appears oddly shaped. Thick and ungainly.

"Fenella says she's at her mom's for the holiday and she's happy to meet your familiar and give him a free checkup if you want to swing by." Harriet holds up her phone screen for Cordelia to read.

As our witch moves closer to my sister, I notice a slight wobble in her step. Crossing realms can't be easy on the body and almost certainly drained her magic.

The magic of the equinox must be the only thing keeping her awake.

"I'll drive you," I announce as I button my fly.

With my pants back on, I ready myself for a debate. Cordelia takes pride in caring for herself—something she's had to do ever since her mother disappeared into an unknown realm over a decade ago.

That's another risk some traveling witches choose to take. Journeying to a realm that's never been explored. Every moment of the trip is dangerous. Is the realm inhabited? By who, and are they violent? Can you communicate? Is there anything to eat? What are the elements like? What about time passage?

Cordelia claims there are a series of test spells traveling witches cast prior to a new excursion to help determine the answers. But her mother disappeared and hasn't returned in all this time.

And I'm worried Cordelia is training herself to eventually follow her mother's route to try to find the woman.

If that day comes, I'm not sure I'll survive it.

"That works." Cordelia's agreement shocks me back to the present moment.

"Really?" The question jumps out before I can catch it.

The witch's mouth quirks in a curious smile. "Are you taking your offer back?"

"No." I pull my shirt on and step forward to offer my arm, as if we were from a different century and heading into a ballroom. "Just expected more of a fight."

Cordelia lets out a world-weary sigh, her shoulders drooping as the air expels from her lungs. The sight of her folding in on herself strikes a spark of anxiety in my chest, and I slip closer, ready to take all her weight onto me if necessary.

"I'm tired," she admits. "But I don't want to fall asleep." Cordelia doesn't explain further, her attention fluctuating between us and a far-off, hazy-eyed stare.

What happened to her in Meztra?

Taking a liberty, I bend to scoop up Honey, settling the lizard on my shoulder before hooking my arm around Cordelia's waist and tucking her into my side.

"Let's go see the vet."

The witch lets me guide her through the house, her body leaning into my chest more with each step.

For her, this must appear innocently supportive. For me, I'm drowning in the intimacy.

Did she walk like this with anyone in Meztra?

Cordelia might have preferred to press her body against one of theirs. Elfish, she described them from tales her aunt related of the foreign plain. Pointed ears. Tall with lean, muscular, hairless bodies. Beautiful angular faces with peri-winkle skin that glimmered in candlelight. Cordelia's voice went dreamy when she relayed the information a year ago, detailing all the exciting aspects of her future destination.

Were the tears for someone she'd left behind?

4

CORDELIA

The rumble of the engine threatens to lull me to sleep, but I can't stomach closing my eyes just yet. Not when I might wake up and realize this—being home—is a dream.

Honey lacks my concerns, immediately curling up on the dashboard, where his golden scales can bake in the sun as he naps.

Are all those UV rays potentially harmful to him?

The Realm of Meztra had two suns, but they never fully penetrated the thick purplish clouds that crowded the sky. At first, I found the twilight effect enchanting. But after a time, I missed my home's blue sky and yellow rays so strong that they felt like a caress against the skin.

Stretching my hands forward, I lay my palms on either side of Honey's sleeping form, following his example and soaking in the sunshine.

"Are you cold?" Denton reaches for the temperature dials but stops when I shake my head.

"I'm warmer than I've been since I left. Meztra is cold." In more ways than one. "Your sweatshirt helps."

Denton grunts, and I watch a pleased crinkle form at the corner of his eye. He likes taking care of people. Me, his sister, his students, his bees.

"How's work going? What day of the week is it? I've lost track."

The double watch faces on my wrist glint in the direct light, where my sleeve has slipped down. I don't need to wear them anymore now that I'm home, but I can't bring myself to remove the precious device just yet. In the end, the four ticking hands were all that kept me sane. They held my hope.

"Today is Wednesday. Harry and I took vacation days. This year is a good group of kids. Rowdy sometimes, but they love to debate. That's the best way to learn about history." Denton turns on his blinker as he talks about his days as a high school history teacher.

The normally stoic bear loves to nerd out on the past. He spends his weekends exploring museums and historical sites and leisurely reading aged documents in dusty archives. Most of the time, he doesn't have a particular project in mind. He simply wants to absorb as much information about the past as he can cram into his beautiful brain.

"Debate, huh?" I sit back and shift my body to fully face the bear, craving the sight of his face as he speaks even if it's merely a side view. "Isn't history set in stone? You just tell them the facts, and they write them down on flash cards and take multiple-choice quizzes."

Denton gives me an intense side-eye, and I'm surprised he doesn't run a red light. "If I didn't know you were joking, I would excommunicate you from my life for that."

A grin presses hard into my cheeks, using muscles that have gone soft with neglect. "Please, no. Anything but that."

He sighs, the sound rumbling from deep in his chest, and he rests a large arm on the console between us. "All right. You can stay."

Giving in to a sudden urge, I wrap my hands around his thick forearm. The limb lies heavy in my grip. Immovable. A glorious weight that'll keep me steady—keep me *here*—as long as I hold on to him.

"Good then," I murmur. "I'll stay."

The tendons in Denton's hand stand out as his fingers clench and release.

We finish the drive in silence, but we're not ignoring each other. At least, I don't ignore him. I study Denton's fingers with their short, clean nails and callous pads. I trace the lines on his palm, as if I knew the art of reading lifelines and defining fate from the creases in skin. The dark hairs on his forearm hold me enthralled, and I pet them, smoothing the coarse coat with short, devoted strokes.

The bear shifter allows me the touches, maybe sensing how much I need them.

I doubt he can tell how much I need *him* though. That desperate craving I've always kept to myself.

When the truck rocks, tires transferring to dirt road, Honey starts awake.

We've arrived. Virginia Henwood, Fenella's mother, lives outside of Roanoke, her house surrounded by forest. She's a leader in the local coven. The head of the Henwood family. Technically, I could claim a leadership role, too, with my mother gone for so long.

The pain of her absence lacks the sharpness it used to. In my soul, in a back corner that knows more than my mind could ever comprehend, I know she's not dead. Beyond that, what she's done with her life is a mystery. Dorthia Vetle loved me in her way, but she was never particularly maternal. My aunt Sandra is better, happy to act as my mentor, but still not overly affectionate.

When I want to feel loved, I go to the Bluebells.

As Denton parks, a gray pit bull charges out of the house, yapping happily. Her round, muscular body jiggles as she dances from leg to leg, waiting for the visitors to climb from the truck. After settling Honey on my shoulder, allowing him to hide in the curtain of my hair if he'd like, I pop open my door and spy a pale, dark-haired woman in a flowing skirt step out from the doorway.

Fenella, the younger Henwood, hasn't changed since last I saw her. Still an intense focus to her eyes, as if she's seeing me but also more, which is probably the case, as she's a seer —able to peer into the past and, at times, even the future. Unlike me and my traveling, I always get the sense Fenella doesn't like her powers.

If I were a seer, I might feel the same.

The dog sits in front of me, panting as her tongue lolls out in a wide canine grin. Her position reads as expectant.

"Daisy wants to meet your familiar," Fenella explains in her husky voice.

The pit bull's tail thumps against the grass as I crouch down, bringing Honey eye-level. My *druzvel* sticks his pebbled snout forward and chatters at the dog, who gives a short yap in response.

"What do you think they're talking about?" The deep voice draws my attention up to Denton's smiling eyes.

"The secrets of the universe would be my guess."

Daisy huffs out another sound and then whirls toward the house and trots past her witch, something about the movement conveying, *Welcome to our house. Come on in.*

Fenella smirks. "We don't live here, and still, she thinks she owns the place." With a wave, she invites us in as well.

Denton offers his hand to help me straighten, which I appreciate. Exhaustion lingers at the edges of all my thoughts, waiting until I let my guard down to push sleep on me.

We follow Fenella to a kitchen with a tall ceiling and wooden furniture that looks old but sturdy. Homey touches fill the space with knitted place mats, hand-labeled jars, a vase with wildflowers, and a counter full of pastries.

"You should take some of those when you go." Fenella points to the treats. "Ostara always puts my mother in a baking mood. And a gardening one. She's out back, planting things." The witch says the last with a twinge of confusion, as if she cannot fathom someone wanting to grow their own plants.

The easy way I read her face has me smiling. The people I spent the last three years of my life with had mastered the art of hiding behind emotionless masks. I crave candor.

The three of us take seats at the kitchen table—a roughly rectangular slab of wood, holding the original shape of a tree —with two long bench seats on either side. Immediately, the dog hops up beside Denton and carefully steps onto one of his broad thighs.

"Daisy." There's an unspoken *tsk* in Fenella's tone. "Denton is not a chair."

The pit bull continues forward, ignoring any chiding that might stop her, eventually sprawling herself across his legs.

"I don't mind."

As his fingers scratch behind her ears, the familiar sighs in contentment, and I find myself dealing with the smallest twinge of jealousy.

What I wouldn't give to have his touch on me.

"Let's see your little guy."

Fenella extends her hands, and I push my inappropriate thoughts aside. I lift Honey from my shoulder, and he doesn't protest the transfer, merely flitting his tongue out to scent the new witch.

"He looks like a bearded dragon. Only a touch larger. And his color is more vibrant."

The vet holds him with careful, strong hands. She runs fingers over his skin, checking the movements of his limbs, and peers into his mouth. Honey takes the examination calmly with a collection of curious chirps.

"They call him a *druzvel*," I offer. "There wasn't a direct translation. I found him—or he found me—when I was visiting the ruins of one of the older civilizations in Meztra."

Even now, I can clearly see the broken towers of shimmering white rocks on the edge of the realm's version of a desert. I'd walked through a crumbling doorway, and suddenly, a golden-scaled lizard scuttled out of the shadows and straight up my leg. In any other circumstance, I would have flailed and tried to knock the strange creature off of me. But when he settled on my shoulder, I *knew*.

"Apparently, *druzvel* are rare. The *Mellza*—the people of Meztra—use them to hunt down precious stones. The *Mellza* I stayed with helped me care for him." No matter the pain of that memory, I keep myself from flinching. "They told me *druzvel* are delicate creatures."

A cool voice in a lilting language slinks through my memory. *"They need specific care. If there is any deviation, he will die. You do not want your familiar to die, I am sure."*

"Maybe most *druzvel* are, but I doubt Honey is." Fenella's response pulls me away from the warning. "I've had Daisy for six years, and she wasn't a puppy when we found each other. But take a moment to examine her, and she appears to be two, maybe three years old."

The dog's tail thwacks against Denton's thigh, as if in agreement.

"The whole time I've had her, she's never gotten sick.

Never needed medication or surgery. I'd like to credit my skills as a caregiver for that, but in truth, I've found the same thing with other familiars."

"What are you saying?"

"From what I've observed, familiars live longer, healthier lives than normal animals." Fenella offers me a firm smile as she sets Honey on the table between us.

She understands my fear. She knows this terror of potentially losing my partner.

"You don't think I should worry? Even though Honey isn't from Earth?"

The vet pulls a dandelion from a vase on the table and holds the pretty weed out to my *druzvel*. "I think you should trust Honey to show you what he needs. Familiars aren't only hardier than normal; they're also more intelligent."

Honey bites into the yellow petals and munches away.

"They don't need to speak to communicate." Fenella's lips twist, and her eyes get a far-off look, as if she's watching a scene only she can see.

I wonder what messages Daisy has given her witch lately.

"So, his diet …"

Fenella blinks, returning her attention to the room. "I'll send you information on the care of bearded dragons. Start with the food they eat. Let Honey decide if he's interested. If his behavior or appearance changes in any way, call me. But I doubt you'll need to."

She runs another finger down Honey's back, and my familiar trills a noise that sounds like *thank you* to my ears. The vet rises from her seat, gathering her long skirt up as she steps over the bench.

"Let me pack you some pastries. We can head out back, so you can say hi to Mom before you go."

I'm about to thank her profusely when Fenella suddenly pitches forward, gripping the kitchen table tight. Before I can think to do anything, Denton is up and around the table. He holds Daisy under one arm, so the dog doesn't topple to the floor, and he braces his other hand against Fenella's back to spot the witch.

Once again taking care of everyone in the room.

"Hey, what's up?" I ask in a careful voice. "Are you feeling sick? Do you need to sit down?"

Fenella gives a sharp shake of her head and then drags in a ragged breath. The next moment, she straightens and offers us a rueful smile. Denton steps back and places Daisy on the ground. The dog immediately goes to lean her beefy body against the witch's leg. The touch seems to lend Fenella more strength as she stands taller.

"Sorry. Visions have been bombarding me today." She presses long fingers against her temples, as if to clear a headache. "Normally, I drink a tea to suppress them. But I forgot it this morning. Then, with Ostara …" Fenella lets the sentence end in the air, but I understand.

Even with my magic depleted from the travel, I can sense the power of the equinox pulsing around us.

"See anything interesting?" I wince. "Sorry. That was rude."

The seer shakes her head and settles back at the kitchen table. Daisy lays her blocky head in the woman's lap. "This one was good. Simple. The future, I'd guess. You with white hair." She offers me a gentle smile. "Honey on your shoulder. And"—her eyes flick to Denton and back to me—"you're surrounded by friends."

Joy rushes through my chest, and suddenly, I'm the one clutching the table. Unless I dye my hair white tomorrow, Fenella's prediction sounds like Honey will survive fine here on Earth for many years to come.

A sob lodges in my throat, and I swallow repeatedly to keep the messy noise inside.

"Your vision"—Denton's voice, rougher than usual, fills the kitchen—"predicts the future? What you saw will definitely happen?"

Fenella's lips pinch, and she keeps her eyes on her hand, where she strokes Daisy's head. "I'm not sure. I've only had a handful of future sightings, and I've yet to live old enough to see if they come true. But I think this means, that future *could* happen."

The bear shifter's face sinks into a frown. He might be unhappy with the vague answer, but Fenella just confirmed a long life for Honey is possible.

That's all I need for now.

5

CORDELIA

Savrellzel's hand claims mine, cool and smooth as marble. Every moment we touch, I feel the blood retract inside my body, seeking to warm my core as it gives up on my extremities.

But the Mellza love to touch me, and I'm so affection-starved that the cold normally doesn't matter.

"I need to find Honey. I know you said he can go anywhere on the estate, but he has never disappeared for more than a few hours. I am worried." My grasp of their language gets better every day, but I know I still sound stilted and overly formal.

"I know of his whereabouts. Come, my star." Savrellzel guides me through towering halls built of stone, veined with precious metals. Orbs evenly spaced along the walls glow with steady light, casting sharp shadows across the Mellza's beautiful face.

"Your sister told me what that means. My star. I think you need to find someone else to gift the title to."

In Meztra, the skies are constantly opaque with clouds, except for one night of the turning. Something in the wind shifts, parting the vapor in the atmosphere for a brief time, long enough to spy clear night sky and one shimmering star.

What I originally thought was a friendly term of endearment turned out to be a deep declaration of romantic affection.

Savrellzel might as well be saying my love.

"If I called any other my star, I would speak a falsehood."

Before I can push again, we round a corner into a wing of his family's sprawling estate I've never visited before. A set of intricately designed doors stand at least twenty feet tall. All doors in this land are larger with the average Mellza standing at least six and a half feet. But even for them, this is a bit much.

"Why is Honey here?"

This doesn't seem like a place that would interest a druzvel. Even though I only found him a short while ago, I've learned so much about my familiar. He's more interested in the gardens than a tucked-away room.

"I made a place for him."

"What—"

He cuts my question off by turning the knob and pulling the door wide, revealing the scene within. My breath catches at the wonderful sight.

An indoor garden. Plants fill the space—glossy leaves, tall stalks, flowering petals. Yes, everything is an odd-to-me shade of purple and blue. Still, I realize how magnificent this greenhouse is in a realm that focuses largely on stone.

"Savrellzel," I gasp, a wave of unexpected gratitude overwhelming me. "You did this? For Honey?"

The Mellza curls his lips carefully, unused to smiles until I explained their meaning on Earth. "For you, my star."

Too awed by the gesture to correct him, I step into the room, eager to search for my familiar. He must be having a grand time in the indoor jungle. I might have to relocate my living quarters here.

"Thank you. Thank you so much."

I pick up my pace, aiming for the small break between two plants, but his grip tightens, holding me back.

"Careful. Do not hurt yourself."

"Hurt myself?" I meet his crystalline eyes. "Are the plants dangerous?"

"Of course not." His answer eases my spark of anxiety. "But you were on a path to collide with the wall."

"What wall?" Turning to examine the room, I search for the obstruction but see nothing. Nothing, except a barely discernible rainbow glitter in the air.

"The wall around the garden."

Horror rises in a slow, sickening glide as I hold out my free hand and step forward carefully this time. In two paces, my fingertips find a hard surface, and I finally see the almost-translucent enclosure.

"Why"—I struggle to keep my voice steady—"is there a wall?"

"For safety."

Just then, the sound of little claws on stones reverberates through the chamber. Through an opening in the leaves, my druzvel bursts forth, scurrying toward the barrier.

"Honey!"

I crouch down, awkwardly because Savrellzel won't let go of my hand, and press my palm against a surface that I instinctively know is far sturdier than glass. My familiar butts his spiny head against the barrier and then desperately scratches at the solid divide, trying his hardest to reach me. The sight breaks my heart and spikes a panicked adrenaline through my veins.

"Shh, Honey. Calm down," I coo, worried he'll hurt himself. "Where is the door? How do I get in?"

When I glance back, hoping to watch the Mellza's eyes point me in a direction, I find only him staring at me.

"You do not."

. . .

I wake up, screaming.

"Cordelia! Cor! Shh, sweet Cor. Calm down."

Warmth envelops me. Heat cradling my body, soothing me.

"Honey," I sob. My eyes shut as I cry, terrified if I open them, I'll see a rainbow glitter in the air that denotes walls fashioned from diamonds.

"Here. He's right here. In your hands. Do you feel him? Hug him close, but not too hard. Don't want to poke yourself."

That last comment has a laugh twining with my sobs, and relief spills through me when I feel the smooth, pebbled skin and small spines of my *druzvel*. Still, the crying takes some time to abate. While the panicked fear slowly seeps away, I focus on the sensations around me to help with the calm. Honey's encouraging chirps. A comforting pressure against the right side of my body. The sweet and earthy scent I long for every day of my life.

Denton. I'm with Denton.

Only when that fact registers am I able to open my eyes, blinking tears away until I meet a concerned gray gaze.

"Bad dream?" Thick brows dip in the middle with his question.

"Bad memory," I correct.

The sun rests high in the sky, and I realize we're on the edge of some woods. Last I remember, we were driving back to his house, but now, Denton holds me in his arms, against his chest, as he crouches beside his truck. I fell asleep after we left the Henwoods' house, and the bear must have pulled over when I started freaking out. The relief of learning Honey can survive on Earth finally giving me permission to relax.

But that left me vulnerable to the memories.

"Do you want to talk about it?"

Speaking what happened right now—with the feel of that impenetrable wall pressing against my fingers still strong in my mind—I can't handle it.

"Can we just sit in the sun for a while? I feel like I'm full of darkness. Like I have three years' worth I need to balance out."

I can tell Denton is trying to keep a comforting expression on his face when, really, he wants to scowl. Not at me though. By now, I know the bear hates the idea of people he loves hurting. He wants to grump my fear away. The thought helps soothe me.

"Course," he says. "I got a blanket in the back. We can get in the truck bed."

Denton gently sets me on my feet, making sure I can stand on my own before he leaves me to set up the back. While he's out of sight, I lean into the truck cab and find a roll of paper towels under the seat. I use one to clean up my face as best I can, but there's no rubbing away the blotchy skin and puffy eyes.

"Come around. I'll lift you up."

Denton's set up a cozy space with a couple of blankets. The warmth of the sun soaks into the fabric, and I settle on the material. Honey scuttles past me, climbing onto the roof of the cab, where he curls up for another nap. The *druzvel* appears to approve of his Earth life so far.

Denton lies back on the blankets, staring toward the sky and leaving me plenty of space beside him to do the same. I fight the strong urge to drape myself over his familiar body, but instead, I lie close but not touching.

When I'm settled, his hand sneaks into mine, lacing our fingers, and I find true contentment.

Denton doesn't pry. The bear shifter keeps quiet, allowing me the peace I need to push away the dark parts of the past.

What makes the memories hurt all the more is that for a long time, I enjoyed my adventure.

The end was the problem.

"When I went through the portal, things were … not easy … but they worked out." *Am I ready to talk about this?*

If I need another day, week, month, year, Denton would give them to me. But I think the not knowing why I hurt, why I cry sometimes, will tear him up inside.

"I roamed around until I found people. The *Mellza*. They remembered my aunt from years back. They liked humans. Thought we were interesting and entertaining. I became friends with a female named Pravrellzal."

Denton grunts to let me know he's listening. A stray cloud floats by but does nothing to obscure my lovely sunshine.

"She was not royalty exactly. More like a VIP. Rich. An elite in their society. But she wanted to go on adventures. So, that's what we did most of the time I was there. Pravrellzal and I explored their world. It's a beautiful place. Cold and harsh but gorgeous. For a while, I was happy there."

"For a while," Denton repeats, not in a questioning tone, but curious nonetheless.

The blanket bunches under my head as I slowly nod. "Things changed when I found Honey, though I didn't realize it at first. Prav said we should go back to her home. That there were adventures to be had in her city. Different sights to see. And she was right."

That time in the city seemed to pass faster than our time in the wild. So fast that I almost lost track. But I never took off my watches. Not even when jewels were presented to replace them. Sometimes I wondered if the gifts were offered in a sly way to pull me further from my home.

"We went to parties and grand stone mansions. She bought me elegant clothes. They all itched though." I scratch my neck against the phantom discomfort. "Their skin was tougher, so the material didn't bother them. But I worked through it and enjoyed myself. So did Honey. He and I were oddities everyone wanted to meet. I got to know more *Mellza*, including her brother, Savrellzel."

There's an almost inscrutable clench of Denton's fingers, and I wonder if I betrayed my feelings from the way I said the *Mellza's* name.

"He was doting and complimentary and tried to court me. I did my best to turn him down kindly, not wanting to upset Prav. But he never took the hint. Then, one day—" I choke and realize a sob threatens to cut off my story. I press the urge away, reminding myself I'm on Earth, with Denton, in a truck bed, soaking up the sun, and Honey is safe beside me.

Nothing bad can happen here.

"What did he do?" The low menace in Denton's voice breaks through my calming thoughts, and I turn my head to see his face has gone hard as he glares toward the sky.

Horrible rainbows sparkle in my memory.

"He built an impenetrable enclosure and put Honey inside it, knowing I'd never leave him." Panic clenches my heart, and I breathe through the tension. "Savrellzel knew as long as he had my familiar, he had me."

A breath shudders out of Denton's chest, and he meets my eyes, his own wide with horror. Somehow, that sight helps.

"Your friend let him do that?"

The pain of betrayal lances through me. "When I confronted her, she told me they were best equipped to keep Honey alive. That I'd never be able to do it on my own. And that she was happy I would be staying with them. That I'd never need to leave."

"They were going to keep you? Cage you?" Rage burns in

his normally gentle gray eyes, and I love him more in this moment than I ever have.

"They tried. But I waited." Holding up my wrist, I show the two watches. One moves at the pace of the realm my body is in, the other always shows Earth's passage of time. Now they move in sync. "When the spring equinox came here, I made my move."

"How'd you rescue Honey?"

I smirk. "I'm a traveling witch. Walls can't keep me out. I knew it would be a risk, using some of my power to portal into his cage before trying to move between realms. But there was no way I was leaving Honey behind. If I had taken him before I could leave Meztra, they might have caught me. But I teleported in, grabbed him, traveled out, and then made for the place I'd first come through. A few miles outside the city walls."

"I thought location didn't much matter when traveling between realms."

The memory of escaping threatens to overwhelm me. Coarse sand spilling into my shoes while chill air froze the sweat on my skin. Fleeing through the wild lands, away from the stony civilization, trying to listen for the sounds of pursuit over my panting breaths.

"If I had been at full power, then it wouldn't have." I reach a hand up, letting the glow of the day play over my skin and reassure me I made it home. "But getting through the diamond wall wasn't easy. The more connections I had to the first trip, the better. Unfortunately, the portal opened farther away than I'd thought, and I was struggling to keep it open. If you hadn't reached through, I might not have made it." I let my hand drop to my stomach. "With my magic depleted and Ostara over, I would have been stuck."

Who knows what my former friend would have done if she'd found I'd tried to escape? I doubt the letter I left, explaining my reasons, would have helped soothe her temper much.

A set of strong arms wraps me up tight, and I find myself in a supportive, comforting embrace.

"I hate them," the bear mutters into my hair. "But I can't fault them for wanting to keep you."

My heart stutters, and I bury my face in his neck, dragging in lungfuls of his honey scent.

If the *Mellza* had succeeded in trapping me, I never would have seen Denton or Harriet again. The thought threatens to bring back my sobbing. Thank the gods they didn't abandon me. That my two friends took the time to set up an altar and wait beside the offerings with no indication that I would arrive.

The Bluebells always wait for me.

"I ask a lot from you," I whisper into the corner of his beard, memorizing the scrape of the rugged facial hair against my lips.

There's a deep grumble that rumbles through his chest and presses into mine. "You never ask me for anything."

When his hold loosens, I swallow a protest.

"And I'd give you so much more if you did."

More. There's a hidden meaning in that offer. One that has me tilting my chin to claim his eyes with mine.

"Like what?"

"Like … everything."

The word lingers between us. A portal to a new destination. One I've always wanted to visit but been too terrified of the dangers from stepping wrong.

Like losing someone who means the world to me.

If I'm going to travel there, I need to know I'm not alone.

Rising up onto my elbow, I stare down at Denton, using my gaze to trace the familiar lines of his face and reacquainting myself with the new scruff of his beard. I like the wild mass. The hint of his animal.

"Everything?" With a subtle shift, I press my entire body against his.

A swallow works through his thick throat as gray eyes burn with unspoken need.

"Everything," he repeats.

"What is *everything*?" Again, I'm selfish with him, requiring his vulnerability before mine.

Denton's fist clenches, then relaxes, and then clenches again, only for his fingers to encircle my arm, drawing the limb to his face, where he places a gentle kiss on my inner wrist. Velvety lips contrast with his coarse beard and set my nerve endings thrumming.

"Everything is everything." His voice drops so low that the sound vibrates in my bones. "But only if you ask."

"Treat me like I'm yours." My plea grows bold under the bright sun, and for a moment, I earn an expression of shock from my bear shifter.

If I'm going to be his, he is going to be mine.

Denton loses his befuddlement, pure hunger engulfing his gaze. His grip on my wrist releases and finds my thigh, dragging my leg over his middle until I straddle him. An iron arm locks across my back, keeping my front tight against his soft yet hard body. There's no retreating from his stare.

"I take care of what's mine." He growls the words, as if angry to admit them.

While the rough tone teases my eardrums, a heavy hand palms my ass, squeezes, and then slides between my splayed legs. Through the well-worn sweatpants, Denton cups my center, pressing possessively.

Mine, his hand says.

My hips rock, nodding in agreement. The weight disappears, and I can't stop a whimper of protest. Unable to look away from my bear's face, I watch the intensity hardening his brow ease into a playful smile.

Yes. I want this version of him along with the firm one. I crave all sides of his personality.

A searching touch slips under my waistband, and the hold returns—only this time, a callous palm rests against sensitive lips.

"Oh!" I gasp, my body jerking once more, seeking as much pleasure as he's willing to give.

"Everything, Cor." Despite the power in his claim, I hear the desperation in his voice. "Just ask."

"I want you." *Am I going to moan? Sob? Melt into the universe from the pressure of needing him?* "You're everything."

Denton slams his eyes shut as he emits a ragged noise. Before I can demand he look at me, a thick finger circles the precious bundle of nerves that overwhelms my brain. For a time, there is just the strumming of his touch and the rising sun of ecstasy in my body. Nonsense noises spill from my throat as he works me, and then I moan low as he seeks the space inside me. Curling, pressing, drawing out my vulnerable ache for him.

Stroke. Tease. Take.

The bear seeks out my orgasm like a skilled hunter, sifting through the ways to caress me until I press my forehead into his collarbone, sob his name, and shudder through the pleasure spasms twisting my muscles.

When I am spent, panting, and warm—so warm—I find the strength to lift my head and meet his eyes.

But his lids are closed, and his face shows nothing but pain.

6

DENTON

*T*he muted light beyond my closed lids proves they are a flimsy shield. The only protection I am able to erect between me and complete self-destruction.

Because how could I survive the rest of my life, knowing exactly how an orgasm paints Cordelia's face?

"Oh my gods."

The twisted disbelief in her exclamation cuts deep, and my nerves pulse in raw agony as she tears herself off of me. When my eyes open, I can't help curling my fist and holding it to my chest, as if she could somehow take the slick essence of her back.

My witch has gone pale, a sicklier color than when she first fell through the portal, and she appears ready to cry again. My insides roil in protest of her unhappiness.

"Cor—"

"Why did you let me do that to you?" she hisses, and I flinch, my mind a mess of confusion.

"Let you?"

"I-I thought you wanted that." Her frantic hand waves to my favorite spot in the world—the small place in my truck bed where I got to hold her like I'd always imagined. "When you said you'd give me everything, I thought it was because you *wanted* everything. Not because you wanted t-to make me feel better or something. Gods. You *hated* it." Tears stream down her cheeks. "I *ruined* us."

At the sight of her misery, I act on instinct, leaning forward to hook my arm around her waist and pulling the distraught woman into my chest.

"What gave you that idea, silly witch?" Maybe I'm an asshole, but I lock my arms tight, trapping her against me.

I would never truly cage her. I know I can't keep her forever. But I'm going to claim her long enough to eradicate her suffering.

"Your face." She braces her palms against my chest, leaning back as far as she can. "You looked like I'd stabbed you."

"You did," I agree, and she gasps. "I'm a fucking bloody mess inside."

My witch smells so good. Sage and sunshine.

I draw her closer and press what I hope is a soothing kiss to her forehead. "Let's take a walk."

"You tell me you're emotionally bleeding internally, and now, you want to go on a stroll?"

Disbelief looks beautiful on her. Every emotion does.

"Yeah. Let's go."

After making sure her clothes are straight, I reach to the roof of the truck and carefully scoop up the napping *druzvel*. Honey lets out a snort but doesn't bother fully waking up. Gently, I slide the familiar into the front pouch of my sweatshirt that Cordelia's wearing.

"Like a kangaroo." I smile at the witch, but she just flicks her anxious attention between the pocket and my face. After another tormenting—for me—kiss to her forehead, I slide her off my lap.

The truck dips on the back axle when I heave myself to the ground. A quick adjustment to the front of my pants, and then I turn to offer Cordelia my hands.

"Denton." She meets my eyes and holds on to me. "I'm sorry. I'm *so* sorry. Things shouldn't have gone that far." With a lithe movement, she hops down, only wobbling a bit on the landing.

"No reason to be sorry." Letting her go hurts like duct tape ripped from bare skin, but I want her to have room to process. And after hearing what happened to her in that other realm, I don't want to take any choices from her. "Will you come with me?" I wave toward the woods.

Cordelia slips her hands into the pouch, and from the way the fabric moves, I can guess she's petting her familiar for comfort. "We should talk about this."

"We will. I promise. But I want to check on the hives."

"Oh." Her tempting lips plump with the sound, and I regret not tasting them while I had her in my arms. "I didn't realize where …" She peers around us, noticing the markers of a place she's been before. "Okay. The hives. Let's go."

And without waiting for my lead, the adventuring witch plunges between the trees, feet on a familiar path.

New buds cover the tree branches as we walk under the reemerging canopy. Small dots of green sprinkled on brown limbs. The air has a fresh rain scent with a teasing hint of humidity, trying to push away the dry winter. Soon, the rustle and crack of the forest floor under our feet mixes with the insistent buzzing of hundreds of insects.

My bees.

We step into a clearing, and the sight of the well-functioning hives both comforts and aggravates me. The structures, full of honeycombs, hold great sentimental meaning while simultaneously bearing me down under the burden of their responsibility.

"Nothing has changed here." Cordelia strolls forward, unafraid of the black-and-yellow bodies swarming in the air. Why would she be? The bees know her.

As my witch reacquaints herself with the hives, I make my normal rounds. Checking there hasn't been any weather damage. Pulling out combs to get a sense of the health of the hive. Examining the perimeter for any animal tracks.

"Everything look good?"

At Cordelia's question, I find her on the edge of the clearing, having retreated. Honey though meanders through the grass, staring up at the little buzzing bodies. Luckily, he seems uninterested in making a snack of my charges.

"Yes." I brush my hands off on my pants and then cautiously approach her.

Cordelia hums with a nervous energy. I'm suddenly fearful the air beside her will split open and she'll disappear.

"Now, can we talk about this? Figure out … I don't know." She finger-combs her hair off her forehead and stares up at the sky, blinking fast. "How do we move past this? What we did—what I asked—gods, Denton. Just because you take care of me sometimes doesn't mean you had to *take care* of me. Why did you?"

If things were different, this moment could be perfect. I could tell Cordelia I love her, always have, and she would tell me the same, and then we'd live happily ever after.

But even if she felt that way about me, there's still the world and who we are in it.

"I did it because I wanted to. And you wanted to. And you'd said I was everything." I shove my hands deep in my pockets to keep from reaching for her. "For a little while, I wanted to believe that."

My witch stares, mahogany brows dipped in confusion. "Why for only a little while? I didn't lie to you. Here I am"— she waves at herself—"telling you that for me, you are every-thing. This is more than friendship." My witch steps forward, closer but just out of reach. "I love you."

"You do," I say as though I knew. But I didn't. There were times I wondered. Every second of my life, I hoped and then hated myself for the pain I embraced. "You shouldn't."

She flinches, and I grit my teeth at my tendency to speak bluntly.

Cordelia scowls at my chest, as if angry with my heart. "I'm sorry for the inappropriate things I've done because of it, but I *refuse* to be sorry for loving you."

Her pull on me grows, the witch's words lingering in the air between us, giving her more mass, more pieces of Cordelia for me to be drawn to.

"I might as well be sorry for the blood pumping in my veins or the magic knitted in my soul. There's no stopping it."

The air shimmers around us—her passion calling to the magic of the day, the universe responding to the sweet sound of her voice, like I always have.

"Cor—"

"I love you." She talks over me, speaking the best and worst words. "I love you without trying, without thinking, without knowing how it started, but sure as all the gods, it will never end." Her glare holds my eyes, burning this moment into my soul. "And I'm. Not. Sorry."

How does one respond to that?

"Harriet is afraid of bees."

Well, probably not that way.

"You have *got* to be kidding me." Cordelia laughs, the sound more exasperated than humorous.

But I'm not changing the subject. This needs to be said.

"Even though these bees would never sting her," I say,

powering on, "she has an anxiety attack just at the sound of them. There's no explaining it. She feels terrible. But she can't come here. She has her butterflies, and I have my bees."

"And I have no idea why I thought baring my heart to you would be a good idea." The witch glances over her shoulder, as if planning to leave.

Get to the point, I urge myself.

"You know these hives were my parents'. That they're blessed by the Earth Mother."

"Yes. I know the story. Two bear shifters got married, and the next morning, your magical hives appeared in the clearing where they said their vows." Cordelia waves behind me to the proof. "What do bees have to do with anything? With me loving you?"

Everything.

"Because I love you too. But one day, you'll leave again, and *I can't go with you.*"

7

CORDELIA

"*I love you too.*"

That's all I need. Everything else is small. Bumps in the road that will try to trip me and might leave my hands scraped raw and knees bloody, but I'll stand and heal, and I'll do it all with Denton at my side.

"You love me too." I can hear the grin in my voice. See it mirrored in his widening eyes, the gray reflective in the bright afternoon light.

"Cordelia. Please listen to me." His grumbly, deep voice saying my name sends shivers prickling over the skin of my lower back and down my hips.

"I'm listening," I say, not bothering to school my face into something serious.

The bear shifter stares at my mouth, and then he tears his attention away and focuses anywhere but on me. For now, I let him.

"The hives might be gods blessed, but they still need

upkeep. My parents are gone, Harriet can't handle coming here, and it has to be a Bluebell. It has to be me." His thick fingers dig into his dark hair, tugging on the strands, as if punishing himself. "Even if I could go with you—and gods, I want to—I can't disappear for months or years. These hives are all that's left of my parents' love, and these bees rely on me to keep them safe and healthy." He turns to me then, the torment in his eyes dimming my glow of triumph. "You shouldn't love me. My responsibility is a cage that would keep you here or a broken heart when you leave."

The normally reserved bear shows me all of his agony and longing, demolishing and reforming my soul with the sight.

"Oh, Denton." In two strides, I cross the space between us to pull his forehead down, resting his heavy head against mine. "I'm not leaving again."

He lets out a pained noise. "Traveling is a part of you."

I press a kiss to one cheekbone, right above his wild beard. "Yes. But I'm done with the other realms." Another kiss to the other cheekbone.

"What about finding your mother?"

"Is that what has you so worried?" I sink my fingertips into his beard until I can caress the dimple on his chin. "I love my mother, but she's not my responsibility. Unless I get some sort of distress signal from her, I wish her well on her journeys. She knew the risks of traveling to an unexplored realm. That's something she craved. Not me. That's not my kind of adventure."

"You've always said how the realms call to you. Like a voice you can't ignore."

His words hold the hurt of knowing he will lose me, and I love him all the more for willingly letting me go.

I've never been surer that loving him is the best choice my heart has ever made.

"The realms weren't calling me." Pulling back just far enough to meet his stormy eyes, I force him to hear the truth of my next words. "Honey was."

The bear's forehead wrinkles in confusion. "Your *druzvel?*"

I nod. "I think my magic knew my familiar wasn't on Earth. That I had to visit other realms to look for him. Because that day, when we found each other in the ruins and I first held him in my hands, all I wanted to do was return here. Come home." If only I had left then, before Pravrellzal and her brother tainted all my good memories of Meztra.

"This is home for you?"

"Of course it is. Why do you think I asked Harriet to set up the altar instead of my aunt or another witch? You two are my family. And I've kept my love for you to myself for the same reason you did. I knew I had to go, and I was worried you didn't feel the same."

My body clenches at the brush of his hot breath finding my sensitive lips and the sweet scent of him in the air. Around us, bees buzz, and Honey chirps to her new friends, but all I want to hear is his voice.

"You're not leaving." The words are a statement, said as if he needs to repeat them to believe them.

I shrug with a mischievous smile. "Well, I don't think all my traveling is done. There's still plenty of Earth I haven't seen. Lots of *historical* sites a certain nerdy bear might want to visit with me. And we'd never be gone for long."

Denton's face clears of disbelief, darkening with arousal. "You're trying to seduce me with history."

I press my hands to his chest, loving the warm softness under my palms. "I'm not trying." My arms slide up, twining around his neck. "I'm succeeding."

In the constant cold of Meztra, I bundled myself in their itchy wool clothes and kept in constant movement to stay warm. But at night, in my bed, covered in blankets, I relied on my imagination to draw the sensation of heat to my chilled skin. My memories cycled through sunny days, hot sandy beaches, steaming mugs, scalding showers.

Inevitably, fiction worked the best. The fantasy of Denton's large body wrapping me in a tight embrace as his heated mouth stole the breath from mine.

Reality surpasses my desperate imaginings.

He tastes of sweet happiness. Our bodies fit together, as if fashioned from one masterpiece. We hold each other up until both of us sink to the springy grass.

Despite my assurances that I'm not going anywhere, Denton tears at my clothes with desperate fingers, as if he's scared I'll evaporate if he doesn't get me undressed fast enough. My hands are just as frantic. I've craved him for too long.

When our coverings are gone, my love sits with his back braced against a tree, me straddling his lap, our eager panting filling the spring air. The sun filters through branches, patterning his skin in gold. I lick him like he's coated himself in honey. One day, I vow to truly soak him in the liquid sugar and consume him, which I must have described out loud from the painful, deep groan he responds with.

"Take me inside you," he begs. "Take me with you, wherever you go."

An easy request to grant, the earlier orgasm leaving me wet and relaxed. I position him, claim him, lock our bodies together, just as our hearts are fused.

"You were always with me," I tell him as I rock, pleasure pulsing from the places his fingers dig into my skin. "Every time I left, I held on to you. I'm not letting you go."

Denton grunts and clasps the back of my neck, pulling me in for another searing kiss while his seeking touch caresses my bundle of nerves. I keen in ecstasy, and my shifter tightens his hold as he bellows loud enough to drown out the hum of the bees.

The warmth of the new season surrounds us, and the magic of Ostara teases the sensitive edges of my soul as I relax in the hold of my bear. Together, we recover with deep breaths and gentle caresses, sharing a laugh when we spy my familiar climbing the tree limb above us. The *druzvel* ignores us, chittering at a yellow butterfly that flutters past.

Finally, I am home.

EPILOGUE

CORDELIA

ONE WEEK LATER

When I knock on the townhouse door, a round of happy barking greets me. From his spot on my shoulder, Honey trills his loudest salutations in return.

A frazzled Fenella opens the door to her home and stares at me with frantic eyes. "Oh. Hello. Do you know what people wear on dates?"

I laugh at the random question completely unrelated to my visit. "Hi to you too. And since I've been living in a different world for three years, probably not. But I'm happy to help."

Fenella turns and waves me inside as Daisy dances around her legs. "I am not wearing the floral dress. It's too cold out." From her muttered volume, I get the sense my fellow witch is arguing with her dog.

As someone who's had long—seemingly one-sided—conversations with a lizard, I don't judge.

I shut the door and head down a hallway that opens to a kitchen. On the clean wooden counter, I set a few jars of honey from the Bluebells' hives. The reason I stopped by. A belated thank-you for the impromptu examination she offered on the equinox.

Now that the holiday is over, the heavy thrum of magic no longer fills the air. I miss the comforting presence, especially because I'm thoroughly burned out. Every time I travel between realms, I need months to recover my strength.

My new mate and I will likely have to wait for the summer solstice before traveling somewhere by magic. Denton wants to take short trips until we know how I do with taking someone with me. But I think I can warm him up to Canada by next spring. My bear would love some maple syrup, straight from a tree. Plus hundreds of miles of wilderness to explore.

"I just saw your text. Thank you for the honey." Fenella strolls into the kitchen, still very much out of sorts, which is odd because the woman I remember from before my trip was always a calm, rational presence. Almost as if she was trying to constantly ground herself in the present moment to make up for the occasions her mind fell through time.

"Which of these blouses looks better? On me. Obviously. Sorry, you knew that." She gestures at the blue silky top she has on and then holds up a maroon option with a bow at the throat.

"Um. The blue?" I pluck the edge of another of Denton's large sweatshirts that I pulled on this morning, hoping she'll realize I'm the wrong person for this job. "You like this guy? Girl? Whoever has you asking the out-of-touch witch for fashion advice?"

Fenella worries her lip as she stares hard at the shirt in

her hand. "A man. He's a professor at the university that I just …" Her eyes lose focus, and I wonder if she's about to have a vision. But Fenella shakes her head and refocuses on me. "I just ran into him."

"Did you *see* something about him?"

The witch's face goes blank. Then flushes red. Then, the color seeps out.

"None of my business." I need to remember that while I'm fine with sharing most details of my travels, the same can't be said of her visions. Seeing the past and future can't always be pleasant. "I'm sorry."

"It's all right." Fenella fiddles with the hanger in her hand as she stares into the air. "Only I don't understand the visions." Her piercing gaze focuses on me. "But the future I saw for you? That was nice and clear. And there's more to it."

"Really?" My throat goes tight. *Maybe we shouldn't talk about this.*

Before the fearful words leave my throat, Fenella continues, "The friends I mentioned—Harriet was at your side, smiling. And Denton …"

"Yes?" *Did this room get stuffy all of a sudden? I'm not sure I can breathe.*

"His arm was around you. He kissed your cheek. Then, Honey climbed from your shoulder to his. There were feelings that emanated off of you. Trust. Affection. Love."

"I love Denton." My breath whooshes out in relief at her description. "We're together."

Fenella offers me her small, confident smile. "That's good. I hope I saw right. That you all grow old and happy together."

"Me too."

Daisy suddenly plants her paws on my hip, reaching her nose toward Honey.

"Daisy! Stop being rude." Fenella tries to grab her familiar's collar, but she's too late to stop my *druzvel* from scrambling down my front, straight onto Daisy's back.

With her new friend hanging on for a ride, Daisy leaves me alone and trots around the kitchen while Honey chitters happily.

Fenella rolls her eyes and then goes back to comparing shirts.

Wanting to give the witch more than jars of honey after the blissful gift of knowledge she just bestowed on me, I venture a question. "Did I hear you talking about a dress?"

Her lips twist. "Yes, but the weather turned cold again. I'll freeze even if the restaurant has the heat on." Still, the witch crosses the kitchen to pull open a door, revealing a tucked-away laundry room. Hanging on the inside of the door is an adorable, long-sleeved black dress, covered in pink and white blooms. The length of the skirt is the problem, appearing to only fall mid-thigh.

"Tights," I suggest. "And a cute jacket." *Wow, look at me. Next stop, The Fashion Network.*

Maybe I'm finally getting my Earth legs back.

Fenella tilts her head, hope appearing in the small curl of her lips as she reexamines the garment.

Daisy lets out a short, pleased bark, and Honey emits a sweet whistle.

"Fine." The witch grins at us all. "This man had better like flowers."

A short while later, I walk into a yard full of real flowers and a bear and butterflies among them.

Harriet raises her head and waves a dirt-covered glove in greeting, unbothered by the chill of the early spring day. "Did she like the honey?"

I nod as I settle on the Bluebells' back porch. "She said she's going to make honey frosting for some cupcakes. She'll send a few our way."

"Yum." My friend holds out her hands as Honey scuttles through the grass toward her.

My little golden lizard has adopted both Bluebells, to the point I'm wondering if bear shifters can have familiars too.

Sharing my *druzvel* with the two of them isn't scary in the slightest.

A warm set of palms settles on my shoulders before a hot kiss presses against the side of my neck.

"I missed you." Denton buries his nose in my hair.

"She was gone for an hour," Harriet teases. "You're so clingy."

As my mate tilts his head to meet my eyes, I see the question in them.

Am I clutching you too tight?

"I like it," I murmur. "The way you hold on to me."

His fingers slide between mine. "Then, I won't ever let go." With a tug, he has me on my feet. "I want to show you something."

As we pass by Harriet, she starts humming the tune of "Can't Help Falling in Love" while cradling Honey against her chest. The sweet notes twine around me in a comforting embrace as Denton guides me into the forest, pulling me toward a future I don't need a seer to tell me will be everything I could have ever hoped for.

DENTON

When Cordelia shivers, I tuck her under my arm, close to my body, and command my body heat to transfer to her. Her strong hold encircles my waist, and I wonder if there was ever a bear as lucky as me.

My guess is no.

"What are you going to show me?" My witch teases her

fingers up and down my side, the press of her nails through the fabric of my shirt tempting me off course.

I can't help myself, stopping us mid-journey to steal a quick kiss. And then another. And then a much longer one that has my heart pounding with wild need for her, as if we haven't spent almost every minute together since her return.

"Mmm," Cordelia hums, her emerald eyes unfocused as she tries to meet my gaze after I break the kiss. "Did you lure me into the woods to eat me up?"

All I can manage is a growl in response, but I force my feet to move again, knowing she'll enjoy the surprise.

A half-mile later, the sound of loud buzzing weaves through the tree trunks. Cordelia lets out a beautifully contented sigh, as if the Bluebells' hives relax her the way they do me. Even more so now that I have no resentment for the way they keep me here. As long as my witch stays, this place will always be home.

We break through the branches into the clearing where my charges live, and my eyes immediately track to the spot where Cordelia and I finally spoke our truths to one another. Where we loved each other out loud. Where I sank into her and began cataloging her pleasure noises.

"Oh! Are there more hives?" She keeps her hand in mine, even as she steps forward, using her free fingers to count. "You added ... five?" My witch gifts me a smile over her shoulder. "Growing the Bluebell honey empire?"

"I didn't add any." And despite knowing the origin story of these bees, I'm still having trouble believing what I found this morning when I came here on my own.

Her brows tilt in confusion. "But there's five more. Right? I thought I counted ..." She trails off, her curiosity melting into wonder.

"It seems the Earth Mother approves of our match."

A new set appeared on their own, like the day after my parents' wedding.

Resting a hand on my witch's waist, I turn her body into mine, pressing her against me and dipping my chin to get a taste. Her lips are sweeter than anything the bees could make, and I suck and nip and groan as she returns my passion tenfold.

"Does this mean"—she pants in the brief moments our mouths aren't joined—"that every time we"—another kiss —"fool around out here"—she's scaling my body now, and I hold her tight to me—"you'll get another batch of magical hives?" Giggles flavor her kisses, proving that she only gets tastier.

"Not sure," I grunt, pulling my witch to the ground with me. "Let's find out."

"Denton." She laughs my name, and I hear love in her voice.

Bees buzz nearby, soft grass cushions my back, hot thighs straddle my hips, and sun paints golden highlights in Cordelia's mahogany hair. For a moment, I'm sure she's used her magic. My witch must have opened a portal into a paradise realm and tugged me through behind her.

But I don't care where we go as long as she keeps a firm hold on me.

The End

～

Thank you so much for reading HOLDING A WITCH. I hope you enjoyed Cordelia and Denton's love story! If you did, please consider rating and reviewing the book. Reviews help other readers discover my books, which helps me make a living and funds my ability to write more romances for you! Do you want to read more magical love stories? Check out the following books for my other witchy romances.

REMEMBERING A WITCH
Seasonal Magic Book 2

Fenella found Graham, the man she's destined to love. Literally. They're both reincarnations of a centuries-old match. Problem is, Fenella's gift of Sight only lets her see glimpses of the long-dead couple and never past a certain point. What happened to the original lovers? Did they meet an untimely end? And if so, are Fenella and Graham headed for the same fate? To get answers, Fenella must give herself over to powers she tries to ignore and reveal her witchy-heritage to the man she's falling for.

WANTING A WITCH
Seasonal Magic Book 3

Roe Fowler never thought the woman she saved six years ago would reappear on her doorstep looking like a golden goddess and offering heartfelt thanks. Roe should have accepted the kind words and waved goodbye. Instead, she invites the vampire into her home. On the longest night of the year, a vampire and a witch will have to confront a painful past and choose whether to let the magic of Yule forge a lasting connection or part when the sun rises.

Keep reading for a sneak peak of the next Seasonal Magic book *Remembering a Witch*, the story of Fenella, a witch who sees visions of the past, and Graham, the ginger haired professor who looks alarmingly like a man who died hundreds of years ago...

REMEMBERING A WITCH

Fenella

When the deep rumble of a man's chuckle brushes past my ears, ducking behind the nearest large object isn't even a conscious decision.

I don't normally take cover at the sound of laughter. Only I've never heard this particular laugh anywhere other than my dreams. The familiar sound fills my mind with memories that don't belong to me.

As I press my back against the rough bark, I am transported away from the pristine university campus, finding myself surrounded by untamed woods.

Sunlight barely reaches the forest floor, filtering through the tall canopy, stingy about which surfaces the rays illuminate. Small bugs flit about, sparkling when they pass through the light. They add a soft hum to the whistle of the breeze between branches. But all these sights and sounds fall away, overshadowed by the man standing across the clearing from me.

His hair, the vibrant color of a ripe pumpkin, shimmers as if the strands were aflame. A friendly grin shows off a set of charm-ingly crooked teeth, which parts to let out another roll of chuckles.

I've always loved making Henry laugh.

No, not me, I remind myself.

Marbella made Henry laugh.

I am not Marbella. Henry is not the man I just heard.

They both died long ago.

I press my fingers against my closed eyelids as if that'll clear the phantom image from my mind. After a moment, the wild forest and the handsome man drift away. As the vision dissipates, I drag in a deep breath to calm my racing pulse.

This is what happens when I break with my routine.

I blink my eyes open and find everything is as it should be. The well-manicured, grassy expanse of lawn in the middle of the local university campus stretches out before me. Stray students meander along neatly paved sidewalks, many in shorts and tank tops on this beautiful, sunny day.

Unfortunately, I remain pressed against the tree.

"So, the man sounded like him," I mutter to myself. "That doesn't mean anything."

As I converse with myself, Daisy sits on her haunches, staring up at me. My surprise vision has interrupted her walk, but she is kind enough to wait patiently as I work through my shock.

I pull in another fortifying breath, planning to take a confident step away from my hiding place, spine straight, head held high.

My body betrays me. Instead, I end up pulling the brim of my floppy hat low over my face and peeking around the trunk.

The owner of the laughter is not hard to find. His flaming hair is a beacon, bright and familiar as Henry's.

I retreat. "By all the gods and goddesses, this can't be real. This can't be happening."

Twigs pluck at the back of my long floral dress as I crouch, as if making myself smaller might somehow lessen the magnitude of this situation. Breathing becomes difficult, air stuttering in and out of my lungs, my body forgetting exactly how to absorb oxygen. My mind, despite being well tuned into the magical currents of the world, never expected to meet Henry anywhere other than in my dreams.

He's not Henry, I remind myself.

Not any more than I'm Marbella.

Another memory rises to the surface, this one my own.

"You are the spitting image of her." My mother holds up a centuries-old painting beside my face, eyes flitting between the image and my teenage scowl with wonder in her expression.

The heirloom is barely larger than my palm. A portrait of my ancestor, Marbella Henwood. The strongest witch our family has ever laid claim to. A woman who died three hundred years ago.

Discovering I was the reincarnation of a long-ago dead woman has never sat well with me. What is a reincarnation anyway? My mother couldn't give me a good answer. Could never say with utter confidence that I was my own person rather than a copy of one from the past.

I've done my best to forget my odd heritage as I live my life how I see fit.

But my magic doesn't want me to ignore anything. The Henwoods are seers. Prone to visions. A pesky skill that showed up the same time I started using tampons. Dizzy spells would hit me hard moments before my mind fell back hundreds of years to watch short scenes from my ancestor's life.

So, Mom taught me to brew a tea filled with a particular combination of herbs that helped suppress unwanted magical interventions.

But at night, with my mind relaxed in sleep, every so often, Marbella's memories will slip into my dreams. Memories of Henry, the ginger-haired horse breeder she fell in love with.

A man who, it seems, has also been reincarnated.

Mom would claim his appearing here, on a campus in Roanoke, Virginia, where I just happened to be walking my dog, was an act of fate. She has always assured me that, with witches, there's no such thing as coincidences.

But what am I supposed to do with this knowledge?

Even growing up in a household filled with magic, I rejected the idea of my doppelgänger status.

Am I supposed to walk up to this stranger, stick out my hand, and say, "Hello. I'm Fenella Henwood. I've dreamed of you since I was a child. Probably because I'm descended from a line of witches, and I believe that you are the reincarnation of my ancestor's lover"?

In that moment, Daisy's patience runs out. Taking advantage of my distraction, she gives a quick tug, and the leash is out of my hands.

"No! Daisy, come!" My whispered command rushes out low and furious.

She ignores it, dancing away.

"Traitor!"

She wags her tail.

Unlike most dogs, who would use their newfound freedom to bolt, my dog sets out at an almost mockingly slow trot. I could catch up to her easily.

If only I left my hiding spot.

Dread settles in my chest as my furry companion heads straight for the Henry look-alike.

I groan, considering abandoning her out of spite.

If only I didn't love the silly pit bull so much.

One more breath, deep and centering, and I follow her.

I have to clutch my skirt, holding it up so the fabric won't tangle my legs, as I sprint after my dog. With my other hand pressing my hat to my head, I'm sure I look ridiculous. As if sensing my approach, Daisy picks up her pace, beelining for a pair of people, the not-Henry one of them.

The familiar man stands next to a blonde woman who spots Daisy trotting toward them. She lets out a squeak before attempting to hide behind not-Henry in the same way as I just used the tree.

I try not to roll my eyes. With Daisy's cropped ears and muscular body, I know most of the world sees her as the embodiment of aggression. But her lack of a killer instinct is the whole reason she got abandoned.

When I found Daisy in the animal shelter, I knew I couldn't leave without her. There was a force, a push and pull, that existed beyond my physical body. She sat still that day as I lay my palm on her soft head. The expression in her liquid brown eyes was more intelligent than I'd ever expected from any animal.

Finally, you found me, she seemed to say.

And I knew, beyond a doubt, she was my familiar. An animal companion brought to my side by the subtle hint of magic in my veins.

"I'm sorry! She's friendly!" I call out. The classic words of an irresponsible dog owner, but at least I didn't *mean* to let Daisy run loose.

To my surprise, the ginger-haired man crouches low and holds out a hand, inviting Daisy to sidle straight up to him. Happiness flutters through my chest at the sight, leaving me more breathless than my short sprint.

When I reach them, I'm panting. Unfortunately, with the

familiar stranger crouching on the ground, I can't even use the wide brim of my hat to hide my face from him.

"I wasn't paying attention, and she pulled the leash out of my hand. I'm sorry," I breathe the words out with my exhale, watching the top of the man's head as he grins down at my dog.

"Don't worry about it. I …" Whatever he was about to say trails off as he glances up and meets my gaze, surprise slackening his jaw.

Does he feel it too? A strange sense of knowing?

This close, I can see he has the same faded blue irises as Henry. But I also pick up the slight differences between the man of Marbella's memories and this flesh-and-blood figure before me. Not-Henry's carrot hair barely brushes the tops of his ears while original Henry let his locks fall to his shoulders. Not-Henry sports a tame beard, compared to the full growth of original Henry.

Still, underneath it all, the face is the same sharply angled shape.

"I'll see you at the faculty meeting tomorrow." The woman who hid from Daisy practically power-walks away, throwing nervous glances over her shoulder.

Not that my dog has any interest in giving chase. She's too busy getting her belly scratched.

Which brings my gaze to his hands. Long fingers, but this set seems almost soft without the scars of hard work Henry sported. I've stumbled upon an academic, clearly.

And I don't approve of the way my heart beats heavy in my rib cage as I watch not-Henry love on my dog.

The woman had the right idea. It's time to flee.

"Daisy, come here. Leave the nice man alone." I give a gentle tug on the leash, and my familiar lets out a pathetic groan.

"Have we met before?" Even as the man rises from his crouch, his eyes never leave my face.

Not sure exactly what the truth is, I offer a vague answer. "I'm not a student here. Just enjoy visiting the campus on nice days."

His head tilts, and some phantom pull in my chest begs me to step closer.

But I am my own person, and I shouldn't have to listen to magical urges if I don't want to.

Problem is, I'm too overwhelmed to sift out exactly which wants are mine and which belong to Marbella.

Distance. I need distance.

This time, when I give the leash a firmer tug, Daisy grunts and rolls to her feet, falling in step beside me as I do my best not to look like I'm running away.

"Wait!"

My body listens to him, even as my mind doubts that I should. There's a set of heavy footfalls, and the overwhelming presence of him comes up beside me.

"Do you mind if I walk with you?"

Keep reading Remembering a Witch...

NEWSLETTER SIGN UP

Get another magical shifter romance for FREE! Sign up for my newsletter to receive *A Selkie's Secret*, a novella that tells the story of Isla, a selkie, and Finn, the human she refuses to fall in love with…

ABOUT THE AUTHOR

Lauren Connolly is a Colorado Book Awards Finalist and an author of contemporary and paranormal romance stories. She's lived among mountains, next to lakes, and in imaginary worlds. Lauren can never seem to stay in one place for too long, but trust that wherever she's residing there is a dog who thinks he's a troll, twin cats hiding in the couch, and bookshelves bursting with the diverse stories written by the authors she loves.